What would your dream pet be?

A snow hedgehog because they're very cute.
— Hope

A flying horse because it could take me anywhere.
— Mia

A magic fluffy unicorn that I can fly on!
— Lola

A ninja guinea pig!
— Harry

A pink otter with invisibility powers.
— Madeleine

Sink your fangs into an Isadora Moon adventure!

ISADORA MOON

Gets in Trouble

Harriet Muncaster

A STEPPING STONE BOOK™

Random House 🏠 New York

For vampires, fairies, and humans everywhere!
And for Henry, the love of my life.

Visit us on the Web!
rhcbooks.com

Educators and librarians, for a variety of teaching tools,
visit us at RHTeachersLibrarians.com

Library of Congress Cataloging-in-Publication Data
Name: Muncaster, Harriet, author.
Title: Isadora Moon gets in trouble / Harriet Muncaster.
Description: First American edition. | New York : Random House Children's Books, 2020. | Series: Isadora Moon ; 8 | Audience: Ages 6–9. |
Summary: Half-fairy, half-vampire Isadora Moon is excited about a visit from her older cousin, Mirabelle, who is half-fairy, half-witch, but when Mirabelle persuades Isadora to take a dragon to school, big trouble is in store.
Identifiers: LCCN 2019051044 (print) | LCCN 2019051045 (ebook) |
ISBN 978-0-593-12622-6 (trade paperback) |
ISBN 978-0-593-12623-3 (ebook)
Subjects: CYAC: Vampires—Fiction. | Fairies—Fiction. | Behavior—Fiction. Cousins—Fiction. | Magic—Fiction. | Dragons—Fiction. | Schools—Fiction.
Classification: LCC PZ7.M92325 Iq 2020 (print) | LCC PZ7.M92325 (ebook)
DDC [Fic]—dc23

MANUFACTURED IN CHINA
10 9 8 7 6 5 4 3 2 1
First American Edition 2020

This book has been officially leveled by using the
F&P Text Level Gradient™ Leveling System.

ISADORA MOON

Gets in Trouble

Chapter One

It was Sunday afternoon and I was hopping up and down with excitement by the kitchen window. My witch fairy cousin Mirabelle was coming to stay! For a whole week!

"It's been ages since we last saw her," said Mom. She was busy baking a special cake just for Mirabelle's arrival. She was using her wand to stir the mixture, and little sparks kept shooting out of the bowl.

"I know," I said. "I've thought of some good games we can play with the dollhouse this time!"

"Lovely!" said Mom.

Suddenly, Pink Rabbit started bouncing up and down on the kitchen counter and pointing his paw toward the window. Pink Rabbit used to be my favorite stuffed toy, so my mom brought him to life with her wand. She can do things like that because she's a fairy.

"She's here!" I yelled. "Mom! Look!"

Mom stopped stirring the batter for a moment, and we watched as Mirabelle swooped down into the front garden on her broomstick. She looked very glamorous.

"I wish I had a broomstick," I said.

Mom gave me a hug.

"Wings are much nicer than broomsticks," she said. She put the bowl of cake batter down, and we both went outside.

"Mirabelle!" I shouted, running toward her and giving her a big hug. "It's so good to see you!"

4

"It's good to see you too!" cried Mirabelle, hugging me back. She was wearing a pointy black hat and a pair of shiny boots.

"Where's Uncle Bartholomew?" asked Mirabelle as we made our way up the stairs toward my tower bedroom.

"Oh, he'll be asleep still," I told her. "Remember, Dad always sleeps through the day. He can't bear the sunlight. He'll be up at seven o'clock in the evening for breakfast!"

But just then I heard a clattering coming from the landing above, and Dad whooshed down the stairs toward us, his vampire cape billowing out behind him.

"Ah!" he cried. "My favorite niece!"

"Hello, Uncle Bartholomew," said Mirabelle. "I like your cape!"

"Well, thank you." Dad beamed. "It's pure velvet!" Dad loves to get compliments.

"Come on, Mirabelle," I said, pulling her past Dad and up the last flight of stairs. "I've got something to show you."

"Ta-da!" I said as I opened the door. In the middle of my room sat the dollhouse. I had covered it with fairy lights. "And look!" I pointed at the miniature dining room. "I've set up a welcome tea party for you!"

Inside the tiny room there was a tiny table, and on the tiny table there was a tiny feast.

"All the food is real," I said proudly. "Even the teeny-tiny sandwiches. They took me ages to make. And look! The sweets are made from cake sprinkles!"

Mirabelle gasped. She picked up one of the sandwiches and popped it into her mouth.

"Peanut butter!" she said. "My favorite!"

"Mine too!" I said happily.

ICE CREAM

We sat down and ate the food together while Pink Rabbit bounced around the room. He was excited that Mirabelle was here too.

"I'll go and fill up the pool with water," I said, brushing crumbs off my dress. Last time Mirabelle came, we'd made a swimming pool for the dolls out of an ice cream tub and a waterslide from plastic tubes stuck together. The slide was attached to the roof of the house and twirled all the way down into the pool. I hurried to the bathroom and came back with the ice cream tub filled with water.

"I also had another idea," I said as I put the tub at the bottom of the slide. "I thought we could make some dolls that look exactly

like us! A Mirabelle doll and an Isadora doll, to live in the house and go down the slide! I have loads of fabric scraps. I think it would be fun. I want my doll to be wearing a black tutu."

"Hmm," said Mirabelle. Her eyes suddenly sparkled mischievously. I could tell she was having one of her "ideas."

"I've got a better plan," she said. "Playing *with* the dolls is boring. Let's *be* the dolls!"

Chapter
Two

"What do you mean?" I asked.

"Let's shrink ourselves!" said Mirabelle. "I'll make a potion. Then we can go inside the dollhouse and slide down the slide ourselves! It will be so fun!"

She got out her little traveling cauldron from her suitcase and started to pour things into it from tiny glass bottles.

I watched and waited, feeling excited and nervous at the same time.

"Are you sure nothing will go wrong?" I asked.

"Of course it won't!" said Mirabelle. She tipped a jar of pink glitter into the cauldron and stirred. I peered in. It wasn't a liquid potion but a powdery one. Mirabelle looked through her suitcase again and pulled out a fluffy powder puff.

"Now let me just dab a little bit onto your arm," she said. "A small bit will only last twenty minutes or so."

I held out my arm, and Mirabelle dabbed some of the powder onto it with the puff.

I sat there and waited. All of a sudden I felt a tingling in my fingers and then . . .

POOF!

There was a cloud of glittery pink smoke, and I landed with a soft thump on the squashy carpet. I was tiny! Mirabelle towered over me like a giant.

"Come on!" I shouted up at her in a high, squeaky voice. "It's your turn!"

Mirabelle burst out laughing.

"Your voice!" she shrieked. "You sound like a mouse!" She rocked forward and backward, laughing.

"Okay, okay," she said. "My turn." She dabbed some of the powder onto her own arm, and there was another POOF of glittery pink smoke.

"Here I am," she squeaked, suddenly appearing next to me. "Look how tiny we are!"

Together we made our way into the dollhouse and up the stairs. We were almost at the roof when we heard a loud thumping sound coming from outside the house.

"What's that?" I whispered, grabbing

on to Mirabelle's arm. "There's something outside!"

We peered out the window, and I breathed a sigh of relief.

"It's just Pink Rabbit!" I said. "Bouncing around. Poor Pink Rabbit—he didn't see us make the potion. He's probably wondering where we are!"

Pink Rabbit looked very confused. He was hopping around and around the traveling cauldron, blinking his beady button eyes worriedly.

I leaned out of the dollhouse.

"Pink Rabbit!" I called in my high, squeaky voice. "Over here!"

Pink Rabbit looked up and saw me. He

wiggled his ears in surprise. Then, before I could say anything else, he jumped right into the cauldron, completely covering himself with the powdery potion. There was a huge POOF of glittery pink smoke.

"Uh-oh . . . ," said Mirabelle.

Chapter Three

We watched the now miniature Pink Rabbit bounce out of the cauldron and across the carpet to the dollhouse.

"What?" I said. "Pink Rabbit won't mind being tiny. He just wanted to join in!"

"It's not that," said Mirabelle. "He covered

his whole body in the potion. He's going to be tiny for days!"

"Oh . . . ," I said, starting to panic.

"Well, there's nothing we can do about it," said Mirabelle as Pink Rabbit came bounding up the stairs and into my arms.

"Let's not worry about it; let's go and have fun!"

The three of us ran up the rest of the stairs and onto the roof of the dollhouse, where the top of the slide was.

"This is going to be amazing!" said Mirabelle. "You go first, Isadora."

I peered down the slide. It looked very steep and twisty from up here. The pool at the bottom suddenly seemed very deep. I had only just learned how to swim underwater.

"It's okay," I said. "You can go first, Mirabelle."

Mirabelle's eyes flashed wickedly.

"Don't be a scaredy-cat, Isadora," she said. "Go on. I DARE you."

I put my foot tentatively at the top of the slide.

"But Pink Rabbit hates getting wet," I pointed out. "I should probably stay up here with him."

"Pink Rabbit won't mind," said Mirabelle. "He can wait here. Anyway, you've got wings; you can always fly off the slide if you don't like it."

This was true.

"Okay . . . ," I said, putting my other foot onto the slide and sitting down. I closed my eyes and held my nose with my fingers.

"One, two, three, GO!" shouted Mirabelle, giving me a little push.

I was off!

"Wheeee!" I squealed as I whooshed downward, twisting and turning, my hair flying out behind me. Around and around I spiraled until . . .

SPLOSH!

I landed in the ice cream tub full of water.

"Wow!" I gasped, coming up for air and spraying water everywhere. "That was amazing!" Just then there was another **SPLOSH** as Mirabelle came flying off the slide and into the water beside me.

"That was SO fun!" she said. "Come on, Isadora, let's do it again!"

I grabbed her hand and we flew back up to the roof. Mirabelle went first this time and I followed her. We tried the slide on our fronts and our backs and going down together. Each time we landed with a wonderful **SPLOSH** in the tub of water.

I was halfway down the slide on my fifth

turn when I suddenly felt a tingling in my fingers.

Oh no! I thought. But before I could do anything, there was a **POOF** of glittery pink smoke.

"Help!" I shouted as my body switched back to its normal size. I landed with a thump on the carpet, crushing the whole slide beneath me. Quickly I picked Mirabelle and Pink Rabbit off the roof of the dollhouse and set them down on the carpet. There was another **POOF** and Mirabelle appeared, full-sized, standing beside me. Pink Rabbit was still the size of a button. I picked him up so he could sit in the palm of my hand.

"The poor slide," I said sadly. I stared at it, crushed next to the dollhouse. "We should have been more careful with the potion."

"You worry too much," said Mirabelle. "We can always make another one."

"I know," I said. "But I'm sad it's broken."

Just then I heard Mom calling us from downstairs.

"Isadora! Mirabelle! Breakfast time!"

I looked at my hand, where tiny Pink Rabbit was bouncing up and down. I couldn't let Mom and Dad see him like that. Carefully I placed him on the bed.

"You take a nap, Pink Rabbit," I said to him. "Hopefully, you'll be the right size when we get back!"

Chapter Four

Mirabelle and I ran down the stairs and into the kitchen where Mom, Dad, and my little sister, Baby Honeyblossom, were waiting to start our evening breakfast. There was a big cake with pink icing in the middle of the table, made specially for Mirabelle.

"There you are!" said Mom.

"You look wet," remarked Dad, glancing worriedly toward the window. "Is it raining? I hope not. I can't bear getting my hair messed up when I go for my nightly fly."

"It's not raining," said Mom, looking at us questioningly. She waved her wand so that our clothes magically became dry.

"Thank goodness for that," said Dad, taking a sip of his red juice. Dad only ever drinks red juice. It's a vampire thing.

"I hope you two haven't been making a mess upstairs," said Mom as she started to cut the cake.

"Um . . . ," I began, thinking about the crushed slide and the water that had been spilled all over my bedroom floor.

"Of course not!" said Mirabelle sweetly as we sat down at the table together. "The cake looks delicious, Auntie Cordelia."

"Thank you," said Mom, beaming. "It's carrot cake."

"Oh, Pink Rabbit's favorite," said Dad with a wink.

Pink Rabbit can't really eat food, but he likes to pretend.

"Where is Pink Rabbit?" asked Mom, looking around suspiciously. "It's very unlike him to miss cake."

I felt my face go hot.

"He's napping," said Mirabelle quickly.

"Ah, yes," nodded Dad knowledgeably. "He's got a big day coming up tomorrow. He needs his beauty sleep."

"Tomorrow . . . ," I said. What was happening tomorrow? And then I remembered. It was bring-your-pet-to-school day!

"Don't tell me you've forgotten," said Dad. "You've been looking forward to it for weeks!"

"Pink Rabbit has been practicing tricks to show the class," Mom told Mirabelle proudly. "He's getting very good at juggling."

"But I thought you took Pink Rabbit to school with you every day," said Mirabelle, confused. "Your class will have seen him already."

"Yes," I said. "But I promised him he could come as my special pet, and the class hasn't seen his tricks!"

"Oh," said Mirabelle, unimpressed. Her eyes glittered dangerously as she munched on her sandwich.

After evening breakfast, we raced back upstairs to my bedroom. "Please, please let Pink Rabbit be his normal size again," I whispered as I opened my door. But Pink Rabbit was still tiny. He was bouncing and sliding up and down the lumps and bumps in my quilt. To him they were like mountains.

"Oh no!" I wailed. "What if he's still like this tomorrow? I can't bring him to school. He might get lost!"

"Well . . . ," said Mirabelle. "I have an idea."

"What idea?" I asked. I was starting to feel nervous about Mirabelle's "ideas."

"How about taking a different pet to

school tomorrow? I could use magic to make you an amazing pet. Something no one will have seen before, something really cool. Like . . . a dragon! Everyone would be so impressed."

"Um . . . ," I began.

"Oh, come on," begged Mirabelle. "Let me do it! It would be awesome!"

"I don't think so," I said. "It's too dangerous. What if it set fire to the school?"

"It won't," promised Mirabelle. "I would make one that didn't breathe fire, just stars and glitter! Oh, pleeeease let's do it. I could make a cute little baby one!"

"Well . . . maybe," I said, starting to feel tempted by the idea. "If it's just a little one."

That night, after Mom and Honeyblossom were in bed and Dad had gone out for his nightly fly, Mirabelle got out her traveling potion kit again. We sat in the dark, and I used my wand as a flashlight so she could see what she was doing.

Into the cauldron went the ingredients of the spell: a pinch of stardust, a sprinkling of dragon scales, a dash of glitter, and a handful of dried flower petals. Mirabelle said some strange-sounding words and gave the potion a stir. We both peered into the cauldron and watched the mixture twinkle in the wand's light.

"Just wait," whispered Mirabelle, "and watch."

The mixture swirled around all on its own. Around and around it went, until it had shaped itself into a ball. The ball grew a tail and then legs and feet and claws.

"Look at its wings!" breathed Mirabelle.

We both watched as the tiny little dragon took shape.

"Oh, it's so cute!" I said.

Mirabelle reached into the cauldron and stroked it with her hand. The dragon nuzzled her finger and squeaked.

"You just need to be gentle with it," advised Mirabelle. "It's only a baby. It needs to be comforted." She picked the dragon up and put it into my lap. Then she jumped off my bed and into her own.

"Good night, Isadora." She yawned. Then she lay down, closed her eyes, fell asleep, and started snoring.

I put the dragon carefully under my quilt and then snuggled down next to it in the bed. It felt strange to have the dragon there instead of Pink Rabbit. I had put Pink Rabbit in a little matchbox bed on my bedside table. I didn't want to accidentally roll on top of him in the night when he was so tiny!

I was just dropping off to sleep when . . .

Squeak, squeak, squeak.

I opened one eye.

Squeak! Squeak! Squeak!

The dragon wanted comforting. I reached out and patted it sleepily on the head.

"Now you settle down," I whispered. "I have school tomorrow!"

The dragon curled up next to me. My
eyes started to close, and my mind started
to drift away into dreamland when . . .

Squeak, squeak, squeak!

SQUEAK! SQUEAK! SQUEAK!

I sat up in bed.

"Shh!" I whispered, hurriedly patting the dragon on the head again and stroking

its little wings. I was worried that it might wake Mom and Honeyblossom.

The dragon stopped squeaking, and I lay back down in bed. By the time I finally got to sleep, it was way past midnight.

Chapter
Five

I still felt tired when I woke up the next morning.

"Rise and shine, Isadora!" said Mirabelle, leaping out of bed and looking as fresh as a daisy. "Where's the dragon?"

I rolled over and peered at her through sleepy eyes.

"What dragon?" I said. Then I remembered. The dragon! Immediately I sat bolt upright in bed and looked around. The dragon had disappeared from my bed, and there was a trail of stars and glitter running out my bedroom door.

Together we followed the trail downstairs to the kitchen.

"Do you know anything about this?" Mom asked, pointing at the glittery, starry floor.

"Well—" I began.

"No!" said Mirabelle. "We don't. We have been sleeping soundly all night." She gave my mom a sweet smile and sat down at the breakfast table. I went to sit next to her, but

I couldn't relax. I felt guilty that neither of us had told the truth.

"Good evening!" called Dad cheerily as he came into the house from his nightly fly. "I mean, morning—sorry!" I heard him taking off his cape in the hallway. And then . . .

"What's this?" he asked, coming into the kitchen and holding his slippers up with a finger and thumb. Glittery slime was dripping from the toes.

Oh no! I thought.

"Something's slobbered on my

slippers!" said Dad, horrified. "I can never wear these again! I can't possibly wear slippers that have been slobbered on! What sort of vampire would that make me?"

"One who cares about the environment," said Mom, tapping the slippers with her wand so that the slime disappeared. "Don't throw them away—that would be very wasteful."

I heard Mirabelle giggle from behind her toast, but I didn't find Dad's slobbered-on slippers very funny. I was too worried about the dragon.

Mom stared hard at Mirabelle and me.

"There's something fishy going on," she said. "I think you two know something about it."

"We don't," insisted Mirabelle. "Do we, Isadora?"

"Umm," I said. I didn't want to lie to Mom, but I also didn't want to look bad in front of Mirabelle.

"I think Honeyblossom must have dribbled on Dad's slippers," I said quickly. "And I saw her with a packet of sequins yesterday. She must have sprinkled them all over the floor."

"Yes," agreed Mirabelle, nodding.

Mom frowned. "What about Pink Rabbit?" she asked. "He's missing again."

"He's in my bedroom," I said truthfully.

"Getting ready for his big day," lied Mirabelle. "He's picking out the best outfit to wear!"

"Hmm," said Mom.

I chewed slowly on my piece of toast. It tasted like cardboard.

"I'm going to get ready for school," I said, hopping off my chair and rushing out of the kitchen. Where, oh where, could the dragon be? Stars and glitter were everywhere! I searched in the downstairs bathroom, the great hall, the grand dining room, and the sitting room, but the dragon was nowhere to be found.

I made my way up to my bedroom . . . and there was the dragon! It was sitting on my bed and puffing out clouds of stars and glitter into the air. It was also three times the size it had been last night.

"It's huge!" I wailed to Mirabelle. "You said it would just be a small one!"

"Well, I meant at first," explained Mirabelle. "It's a magic dragon, you see. It will only last for a day and then disappear." She looked at the clock on my wall. "It's probably a teenager by now."

"A teenager!" I squeaked. "I can't take a teenage dragon to school!"

"Of course you can!" insisted Mirabelle. "All your friends will be amazed!"

"I guess," I said, walking to my closet and taking out my school uniform. "But I wish you were coming too. I don't know how I'm going to look after it on my own."

"You'll be fine," said Mirabelle breezily.

"And there's no way I'm coming to school
with you today. Not on my vacation! Just
relax, Isadora."

"Okay," I sighed, wishing that I was on
vacation too. Witch schools and human

schools have very different holidays. I chose to go to a human school even though I am a vampire-fairy.

I tried very hard to relax as I put on my school uniform and kissed Pink Rabbit goodbye on the top of his miniature head. When I was ready, I found a belt and tied it around the dragon's neck to make a leash.

"Now I just have to get the dragon out of the house without Mom and Dad seeing it," I said.

"Easy," said Mirabelle. "You can fly out your bedroom window. The dragon has wings too, remember! I'll tell your mom that you were running late for school and had to rush. I'll tell her Pink Rabbit was having trouble deciding which outfit to wear."

Pink Rabbit shook his head crossly at Mirabelle from the bedside table.

"No, don't blame it on Pink Rabbit!" I said hurriedly. "Poor Pink Rabbit!"

I took the end of the belt and led the dragon toward the window.

"Goodbye!" said Mirabelle cheerfully.

I stepped out the window into the air and flapped my wings. I gave a tug on the leash, and the dragon followed, leaping out into the morning sunshine. It felt strange to be without Pink Rabbit. And I felt a little sad that I hadn't said goodbye to Mom and Dad, but I didn't know what else to do.

Chapter Six

Together the dragon and I flew over the town and toward the school. As we got closer I could see some of my friends standing in the playground with their pets.

"Hey, look!" shouted Oliver, pointing upward. "There's Isadora!"

"Hi, Isadora!" called Zoe.

"Wow!!" cried Samantha.

"She's brought a DRAGON!" yelled Sashi.

I landed in the playground with the dragon, and everyone immediately gathered around.

"That's amazing!" said Jasper.

"Incredible!" agreed Bruno.

"Whoa!" said Zoe.

The dragon smiled proudly and puffed out a cloud of stars and glitter. Its scales shimmered in the sunshine. I suddenly felt very happy that I had brought such an interesting pet to school.

"Do you want to go for a ride?" I asked my friends. "I'm sure the dragon wouldn't mind."

"Yes!!" cried Bruno. "I want a ride. Let me go first!"

He hopped onto the dragon's back, and the dragon flew up into the air. It flew around in a small circle and then landed gently back on the ground.

"Wheee!" squealed Bruno.

"I want a turn!" shouted Oliver.

One by one my friends took a ride on the dragon's back. When Miss Cherry spotted us, she came racing into the playground, looking very shocked and surprised.

"What's going on?" she shrieked. "This is a health and safety hazard! Everyone, come inside immediately!"

The dragon flapped back down to the ground, and we all followed Miss Cherry into the classroom.

I sat down at my desk, and the dragon sat next to me. It kept puffing out clouds of stars and glitter into the air. The boy sitting in front of me began to sneeze.

"Now," said Miss Cherry from the front

of the class, "we are all going to take turns. Everyone will have a chance to come up to the front of the class and talk about their pet. Who wants to go first?"

Bruno's hand shot up into the air, and Miss Cherry called him to the front.

"This is George the iguana," said Bruno, holding out a large lizard-like creature for everyone to see. "He has a—a—*achoo!*—

a striped tail and—*achoo!*—he needs to be kept warm."

"Wonderful," said Miss Cherry. *"Achoo!"*

Bruno continued talking about his iguana, but he was finding it difficult to breathe. The air was becoming thick with stars and glitter. It wasn't long before everyone in the classroom was sneezing. Glitter can be very itchy when it gets up your nose!

"Oh dear!" said Miss Cherry through sneezes. "I think you should go next, Isadora, and then maybe take the dragon outside for a little while."

I walked up to the front of the class. The

dragon followed me excitedly, wagging its scaly tail.

"Um," I began, feeling shy. "This is—*achoo!*—a dragon!"

The dragon hopped up and down next to me. It started to flap its wings proudly.

"Dragons like . . . umm . . . ," I continued, realizing that actually I didn't know much about dragons at all. *"ACHOO!"*

The dragon flapped its wings harder, disturbing a box of art supplies next to Miss Cherry's desk. Pencils and crayons exploded into the air.

"I think—" began Miss Cherry. But at that moment, the dragon knocked over cans of paint, which fell over and burst open, spattering paint up the walls and all over the floor.

"Um . . . ," I continued, starting to panic.

The dragon was extremely excited now.

It rose up into the air and tried to fly around the room, knocking over anything in its path. Zoe's puppy began to bark and leap across the desks. Samantha's Siamese cat started to yowl. Jasper's snake hissed and slithered away from him.

"Aargh!" screamed Samantha, jumping up on top of her desk. "The snake is on the loose!"

Ten seconds later, the classroom was in chaos.

"HELP!" shrieked Samantha.

"Where's my snake?" shouted Jasper.

"STOP!" I yelled at the dragon.

But the dragon didn't want to stop. It was enjoying itself too much.

"Oh my goodness!" wailed Miss Cherry with her head in her hands.

I didn't know what to do. The dragon was destroying the classroom. Around and around it went, wrecking everything in its path. There was nothing else I could do. . . .

I opened the window.

As soon as the dragon sensed the fresh air, it launched itself toward the window. *Flap, flap, flap* went its shimmery, scaly wings, and my hair blew back in the breeze. Stars and glitter swirled around the room.

And then it was gone. It flew out across the playground and up into the sky, my belt still tied around its neck. I hoped that it would fly far away and never come back.

Chapter Seven

I closed the window quickly so that none of the other pets could escape. Miss Cherry breathed a sigh of relief, but she looked very upset.

"Isadora Moon!" she cried.

I felt my face go red. I had never been in trouble at school before.

"Bringing a dragon to school was an irresponsible thing to do. A dragon is not an appropriate pet for the classroom."

"I'm sorry," I said, hanging my head in shame. "I just—"

"You will go to the principal's office and call your parents," said Miss Cherry. "Tell them what's happened so they can help you find your dragon. Then come back here and help clean up."

I felt like crying as I made my way across the room to the door. Zoe patted my arm gently as I walked past her.

"It's okay," she whispered.

"Don't worry," whispered Bruno. "I've been sent to the principal's office."

But I had never been sent to the principal's office before. I felt so awful. I left the classroom and walked across the lunchroom toward the office. I knocked on the door.

"Come in," called a high, tinkly voice.

I went into the room and saw Miss Valentino sitting behind her desk wearing her usual pair of pink horn-rimmed glasses. Miss Valentino was the school principal.

"What can I do for you, Isadora Moon?" she asked with a beaming smile. "Have you got another gold star?"

I gulped and felt my eyes prick with tears.

"I got in trouble," I whispered. "Miss Cherry told me to come and call my parents."

Miss Valentino frowned.

"Oh dear," she said. "That's not like you. What happened?"

I explained about Mirabelle and the dragon, and Miss Valentino nodded.

"You've got yourself into quite a pickle, haven't you?" she said. "I think it might be time to stand up to that cousin of yours."

She picked up the phone and called my mom.

"Ah, Mrs. Moon!" I heard her say. "This is Miss Valentino. I'm the principal at Isadora's school. I'm afraid I have to ask you to come to the school right away. . . . Mmm . . . Yes . . . yes, she's fine. . . . Well, I'll let Isadora explain for herself. Okay . . . goodbye, Mrs. Moon!" She put the phone down and smiled at me.

"It's all right, Isadora," she said kindly. "Everything will be okay."

It only took Mom ten minutes to arrive

at the school. She must have flown there at top speed.

"What's happened?" she asked. "Is everything okay? And where's Pink Rabbit?"

"I—" I began. "I—" Suddenly, I couldn't bear to tell Mom what had happened.

"I have a stomachache," I lied. "Can I come home? Zoe said she would bring Pink Rabbit home for me later."

I felt bad about lying, and I wasn't sure Mom would believe me about Pink Rabbit, but she just nodded and said, "Poor you. What a shame! We'd better get you home." She let Miss Valentino know that we were leaving. Then she took my hand, and we both rose up into the air, flapping our wings.

Chapter Eight

Mirabelle was in the kitchen when we got home. I saw she had been making moon- and star-shaped cookies with Mom. They must have had a fun day together.

"Oh, yum," I said, reaching for one.

"Not for you," said Mom, swiping my hand away gently. "Not if you have a stomachache!" She filled a glass with fizzy water for me instead.

"Where's the dragon?" whispered Mirabelle as soon as Mom's back was turned.

"It flew away," I whispered. "Shh!"

I spent the rest of the afternoon sitting in the kitchen with Mom and Mirabelle, watching them decorate the cookies and sipping my fizzy water. I went up to my

bedroom a couple of times to check on Pink Rabbit, but he was still tiny.

By evening breakfast, Pink Rabbit still had not returned to his normal size.

"I thought you said Zoe was dropping off Pink Rabbit," said Mom as she put sandwiches and cakes on the table.

"She did," said Mirabelle quickly. "Earlier. You were upstairs with Honeyblossom. Pink Rabbit is having a nap; he's tired after his busy day."

"Pink Rabbit seems to be having a lot of naps lately," said Dad suspiciously.

"Yes," agreed Mom, staring at me quizzically. "He does . . ."

"DELICIOUS sandwiches, Auntie Cordelia!" said Mirabelle in a louder voice than usual. "Really yummy."

"Oh, thank you, Mirabelle," said Mom, delighted. "They're special fairy ones. They change flavor every time you take a bite."

"I thought so," said Mirabelle. "Mmm! Chocolate spread and raspberry jam!"

I put a sandwich on my plate and nibbled at it. I was feeling worse and worse about all the lies we had been telling Mom and Dad. If only Pink Rabbit would return to his normal size!

But then I heard something that made my blood run cold. A clanging, crunching, gushing sound coming from upstairs. The sort of sound a dragon might make if it had been let loose in the house. . . .

"What on earth is that?" said Mom.

"I have absolutely no idea!" said Dad, standing up and swishing his cape around him. "Let's go and look. Maybe it's a burglar." He picked up his glass of red juice. "I will throw this on the burglar," he announced. "It will surprise him."

Mom picked up her wand. "I think this might be more useful in this situation," she said.

Mirabelle picked up her fork and held it in front of her.

"How exciting," she said. "I will poke the burglar with my fork!"

We all ran up the stairs to the bathroom. I tried to get there first, but with his super-speedy vampire cape, Dad was a lot faster than I was.

"WHAT'S THIS?!" I heard him gasp as he walked into the room.

The dragon was sitting in the bathtub, and it had half a water pipe in its mouth, which it had ripped out from beneath the sink. Water was gushing all over the bathroom floor, and stars and glitter swirled everywhere. Mom waved her wand to stop the water temporarily.

"We'll have to call a plumber," she said. Then she narrowed her eyes at me.

"Isadora Moon," Mom said in a stern voice. "I do believe that is your belt tied around that dragon's neck."

I hung my head.

"What's going on?" asked Dad with

his hands on his hips. "I thought you were behaving strangely, Isadora."

"Very strangely," agreed Mom. "All this lying and sneaking around."

"I'm sorry," I said in a small voice. Mirabelle stood quietly behind me.

"Now answer me honestly," said Mom. "Is this Pink Rabbit in the bathtub? Have you turned him into a dragon? Is this why we haven't seen him lately?"

"No!" Mirabelle giggled. "That's not Pink Rabbit!"

Mom didn't find it very funny.

"Pink Rabbit is napping," said Mirabelle again. "He's—"

But I couldn't bear to tell any more lies.

Chapter Nine

"He's not napping," I said to Mom and Dad.
"He's turned into a miniature rabbit."

"What?!" said Dad.

"We made a potion," I continued, "and Pink Rabbit jumped into it and is now really tiny. And I crushed my dollhouse slide when I grew big again, and then we made

another potion so that I would have a really
interesting pet to take to school. A dragon.
But the dragon just made a mess everywhere,
so I blamed it on Honeyblossom. Then the
dragon got me into trouble at school ...

but it had flown away, so I told you I had a stomachache so I wouldn't have to tell you what really happened, which is that the dragon made a mess in my classroom and I was supposed to help clean up. I'm sorry."

"I see," said Dad, looking disappointed. Mom shook her head, and I started to cry. Mirabelle stood there, not saying a word.

"You are grounded for a week," said Dad. "Literally. No more flying. No more magic and no more peanut butter sandwiches!"

"Yes," agreed Mom. "All this lying! What sort of example are you setting for your cousin?"

I sniffed sadly.

Then Mirabelle spoke up. Her face had gone very red.

"Um," she said, "it's not all Isadora's fault." Then she started to explain. "Really, it's mostly my fault," she said, looking down at the floor. "I persuaded her to do everything. Isadora didn't want to make the dragon or take it to school. She wasn't even very excited about making the shrinking potion. I'm sorry too."

"I see," said Mom quietly.

"Hmm," said Dad.

They both turned to me.

"Isadora," said Mom, "you need to learn to stand up for yourself."

"You shouldn't do things you don't want to do just because someone else tells you to," said Dad.

"I know," I said in a small voice.

"And, Mirabelle," said Dad, "you should know better! You are older than Isadora. We don't want any more lying this week."

"Okay," said Mirabelle meekly.

"Well then," said Mom, brightening. "Let's put this behind us."

"But you're still grounded," added Dad

cheerfully as he took hold of my belt and led the dragon out of the bathroom. "BOTH of you."

We all went back downstairs with the dragon and finished our evening breakfast. The dragon must have been very hungry because it ate all the sandwiches and then gobbled down all the cake. It even drank a glass of Dad's red juice.

"Poor thing," said Mom.

After evening breakfast, Mirabelle and I went back to my bedroom with the dragon, which was now almost the size of a car! Pink Rabbit was sitting on the bed . . .

And he was normal size!

"Oh, Pink Rabbit!" I said, hugging him tightly to my chest. "You're back to yourself again!" Pink Rabbit squirmed happily in my arms and wiggled his ears. The dragon flapped its wings.

"It's probably a very old dragon now," observed Mirabelle, giving its snout a gentle pat. "Probably about one hundred years old!"

"It has a lot of energy," I said. "Do you think it needs to fly before bedtime?"

"Maybe," said Mirabelle, opening the window. "Shall we go for a last ride on its back before it disappears?"

"I don't know," I said. "Dad did say no more flying for a week."

"Oh yes," said Mirabelle with a naughty glint flashing in her eyes. "Well, we wouldn't really be flying, would we? The dragon would be flying."

She had a point. I did want to go for a last fly on the dragon. And not just because Mirabelle wanted to.

"Okay," I agreed. "Let's go. But I'm going because I want to. Not because you think it's a good idea."

We both climbed onto the dragon's back, and I held Pink Rabbit tightly to my chest. The dragon happily puffed a cloud of stars and glitter out of its snout. Then it launched itself out the window and into the starry sky.

"That was wonderful!" I said when we got back to my bedroom.

"It was," agreed Mirabelle.

The dragon yawned and curled up on my floor. Mirabelle and I both got into bed, and I turned out the light.

"Good night, dragon," we whispered.

When we woke up the next morning, the dragon had gone. There was just a pile of stars and glitter on the floor. I felt a little sad.

"It's okay," said Mirabelle, patting me gently on the arm. "I can make you another one."

"No!" I said firmly. "Absolutely not."

"But—" said Mirabelle.

"No," I said.

Then I hopped out of bed and pulled my dollhouse into the middle of the floor.

"Let's play my game today," I said. "After breakfast, let's make dolls that look like us. I think that would be really fun!"

I got out my box of fabric scraps.

"We don't even need any magic to do it,"
I said happily. "We can make them the old-
fashioned way. Mine will have a black tutu."

"Okay," said Mirabelle, starting to sound
excited. "Can mine have some little pointed
black boots?"

"Of course it can," I said. "That would look amazing! We can make a tiny Pink Rabbit too."

Together we went down the stairs to breakfast, Pink Rabbit bounding along behind us.

"You know what would be fun," said Mirabelle, her eyes glinting again. "If we used magic to bring the dolls to life! We could—"

"No," I said firmly. "We're not going to do that, Mirabelle."

"Okay," said Mirabelle meekly.

"It will be fun anyway. I promise!" I said. And it was.

Are you more fairy or more vampire?
Take the quiz to find out!

What's your favorite color?

A. pink   B. black   C. I love them both!

Would you rather go to:

A. a glittery school that teaches magic,
ballet, and making flowery crowns?

B. a spooky school that teaches flying, bat training,
and how to have the nicest hair possible?

C. a school where everyone gets to be totally
different and interesting?

On your camping trip, do you:

A. put up your tent with a wave of your
magic wand and go exploring?

B. pop up your fold-out four-poster bed
and avoid the sun?

C. splash around in the water and have a great time?

RESULTS

Mostly As
You are a glittery, dancing fairy and you love nature!

Mostly Bs
You are a sleek, caped vampire and you love the night!

Mostly Cs
You are half-fairy, half-vampire and totally unique—just like Isadora Moon!

Family Tree

My mom,
Countess Cordelia
Moon

Baby Honeyblossom

My dad,
Count Bartholomew
Moon

Me!
Isadora Moon

Pink Rabbit

Sink your fangs into another Isadora Moon adventure!

"Even fairies have to go to school," said Mom.

"Vampires too!" added Dad.

"But I don't *want* to go to school," I said. "I have a perfectly busy and fun life at home with Pink Rabbit."

"But you might enjoy it," insisted Dad. "I used to love my vampire school as a young boy."

"And I adored my fairy school!" said Mom, spooning some flower-nectar yogurt into her bowl.

"You'll have a wonderful time!" They both smiled.

I wasn't so sure.

"But I'm not a full fairy," I said. "And I'm not a full vampire. So which school would I go to? Is there one especially for vampire-fairies? Is there a school for me?"

"Well . . . no," said Mom. "Not exactly."

"You are very rare," said Dad.

"But very special!" added Mom quickly. "And I think fairy school would suit you perfectly."

"But of course you may prefer vampire school," said Dad. "It's a lot more exciting."

Every Isadora Moon
adventure is totally unique!

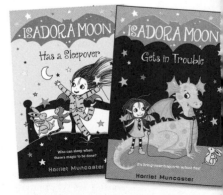